Jingle Bells

as told and illustrated by Iza Trapani

 SCHOLASTIC INC.

New York Toronto London Auckland Sydney
Mexico City New Delhi Hong Kong Buenos Aires

Dashing through the snow
In a one-horse open sleigh,
O'er the fields we go,
Laughing all the way.
Bells on bobtail ring,
Making spirits bright.
What fun it is to ride and sing
A sleighing song tonight!

Oh, jingle bells, jingle bells,
Jingle all the way.
Oh, what fun it is to ride
In a one-horse open sleigh!

Soaring through the sky
On a magic ride,
In our sleigh we fly,
Traveling far and wide.
We can hardly wait
To see and to compare
How other countries celebrate
The Christmas season there.

Oh, jingle bells, jingle bells,
Jingle with delight.
Let's go tour around the world
On this happy night!

Here in Mexico
There's no need to be glum.
All the children know
Candy's sure to come.

Bearded little gnomes
Bearing gifts and toys
Are often hiding in the homes
Of Swedish girls and boys.

Oh, jingle bells, jingle bells,
Jingle in the air.
Christmastime is so much fun
For children everywhere!

See the folks parade
In the Philippines.
Lanterns that they made
Light the cheerful scene.

Polish families
Feast by candlelight.
The meal begins when someone sees
The first star of the night.

Oh, jingle bells, jingle bells,
Jingle merrily.
Christmas is a special time
For friends and family.

Kids in Italy
Find it hard to snooze
Knowing there might be
Presents in their shoes.

What a lovely treat!
In Kenya we can hear
The sound of voices soft and sweet
Spreading Christmas cheer.

Oh, jingle bells, jingle bells,
Jingle as we ride.
Christmas is a happy time
With good friends by our side!

Dashing through the snow
As our journey ends,
To our home we go,
With our newfound friends.
By the firelight
Good times we will share,
And bid warm wishes on this night
To people everywhere!

Oh, jingle bells, jingle bells,
Jingle loud and clear.
Merry Christmas, peace on earth,
And a wonderful New Year!

Christmas Traditions

Christmas greetings in Spanish: *Feliz Navidad!*

Las Posadas is a Mexican tradition in which people celebrate by visiting different houses in their neighborhood. They are invited inside for goodies and punch, and the children take turns breaking a *piñata* (a papier-mâché star, donkey, or other animal). When the *piñata* breaks, candy and small gifts spill out.

Christmas greetings in Swedish: *God Jul!*

In Sweden children believe that a gnome called a *tomte* lives under the floorboards of their home or barn. He usually comes out for a visit after the Christmas feast, carrying a big sack of gifts and toys. Children often leave a bowl of rice pudding outside for the *tomte*.

Christmas greetings in Pilipino: *Maligayang Pasko!*

In the Philippines there are processions through the towns at night. Colorful star-shaped lanterns called *parols* are carried through the procession and also hang from the doors and windows of homes. Many of these lanterns are homemade. Each town is lit up with a warm glow.

Christmas greetings in Polish: *Wesołych Świąt!*

In Poland on Christmas Eve, which is called *Wigilia*, families gather together for a big twelve-course meal that consists of mostly fish, noodle, and vegetable dishes. When the first star of the night is seen, families light their candles and Christmas trees and sit down to feast. There is always an extra place set in case a visitor comes.

Christmas greetings in Italian: *Buon Natale!*

In Italy children expect a visit from *la Befana*, an old woman with a broom. The legend is that *la Befana* was too busy sweeping her house to bring gifts to baby Jesus on time. To make up for this, she now visits homes at Christmastime, bringing presents and sweets for all children. She puts them inside the shoes that they leave out for her (their biggest pair, of course!).

Christmas greetings in Swahili: *Krismasi Njema!*
English is also an official language in Kenya, so many people just say "Merry Christmas!"

At night in Kenya carolers go door to door in the village. At each home they visit, people offer them small gifts or money that they in turn give to their churches on Christmas Day. The churches in Kenya are decorated with balloons, flowers, and even Christmas trees.

Jingle Bells

Dash-ing through the snow In a one-horse op - en sleigh, O'er the fields we go, Laugh-ing all the way.

Bells on bob - tail ring, Mak-ing spi-rits bright. What fun it is to ride and sing A sleigh-ing song to-night! Oh,

jin - gle bells, jin - gle bells, Jin - gle all the way. Oh, what fun it is to ride In a one-horse op - en sleigh!

Soaring through the sky
On a magic ride,
In our sleigh we fly,
Traveling far and wide.

We can hardly wait
To see and to compare
How other countries celebrate
The Christmas season there.

Oh, jingle bells, jingle bells,
Jingle with delight.
Let's go tour around the world
On this happy night!

Here in Mexico
There's no need to be glum.
All the children know
Candy's sure to come.

Bearded little gnomes
Bearing gifts and toys
Are often hiding in the homes
Of Swedish girls and boys.

Oh, jingle bells, jingle bells,
Jingle in the air.
Christmastime is so much fun
For children everywhere!

See the folks parade
In the Philippines.
Lanterns that they made
Light the cheerful scene.

Polish families
Feast by candlelight.
The meal begins when someone sees
The first star of the night.

Oh, jingle bells, jingle bells,
Jingle merrily.
Christmas is a special time
For friends and family.

Kids in Italy
Find it hard to snooze
Knowing there might be
Presents in their shoes.

What a lovely treat!
In Kenya we can hear
The sound of voices soft and sweet
Spreading Christmas cheer.

Oh, jingle bells, jingle bells,
Jingle as we ride.
Christmas is a happy time
With good friends by our side!

Dashing through the snow
As our journey ends,
To our home we go,
With our newfound friends.

By the firelight
Good times we will share,
And bid warm wishes on this night
To people everywhere!

Oh, jingle bells, jingle bells,
Jingle loud and clear.
Merry Christmas, peace on earth,
And a wonderful New Year!

For Dana and Danny, two precious little stars
—I. T.

ISBN-13: 978-0-439-92426-9
ISBN-10: 0-439-92426-X

12 11   13 14 15 16/0

Printed in the U.S.A.   40

First Scholastic printing, December 2006

Illustrations done in watercolor

Display type and text type set in Pink Martini and Edwardian

Production supervision by Brian G. Walker

Designed by Diane M. Earley